CoComelon™

5-MINUTE STORIES

Simon Spotlight
New York London Toronto Sydney New Delhi

SIMON SPOTLIGHT

An imprint of Simon & Schuster Children's Publishing Division

1230 Avenue of the Americas, New York, New York 10020

This Simon Spotlight edition December 2022

For information about special discounts for bulk purchases, please contact Simon & Schuster Special Sales at 1-866-506-1949 or business@simonandschuster.com.

Manufactured in China 0822 WGL

10 9 8 7 6 5 4 3 2 1

ISBN 978-1-6659-2600-3

ISBN 978-1-6659-2601-0 (ebook)

These titles were previously published individually by Simon Spotlight with slightly different text and art.

CONTENTS

HELLO, NEW FRIEND!

Hello, new friend!
Hello, new friend!
What's your name?

Hi, everybody! My name is JJ. This is my puppy, Bingo. He is my best friend!

I like to play with the toy shark at school!
Chomp, chomp, chomp!

Hello, new friend!
Hello, new friend!
What's your name?

Hello! I am JJ's mom.
I teach JJ lots of things—like how to play soccer!

And I am JJ's dad. Hello! JJ and I do lots of fun things together—like playing the guitar!

Nice to meet you,
nice to greet you,
say hello!

Hello, new friend!
Hello, new friend!
What's your name?

Hi, everybody! My name is TomTom. I am JJ's big brother. I am teaching him how to read!

Nice to meet you,
nice to greet you,
say hello!

Hello, new friend!
Hello, new friend!
What's your name?

Hello! My name is YoYo.
I am JJ's big sister.
We love to do arts and crafts together!

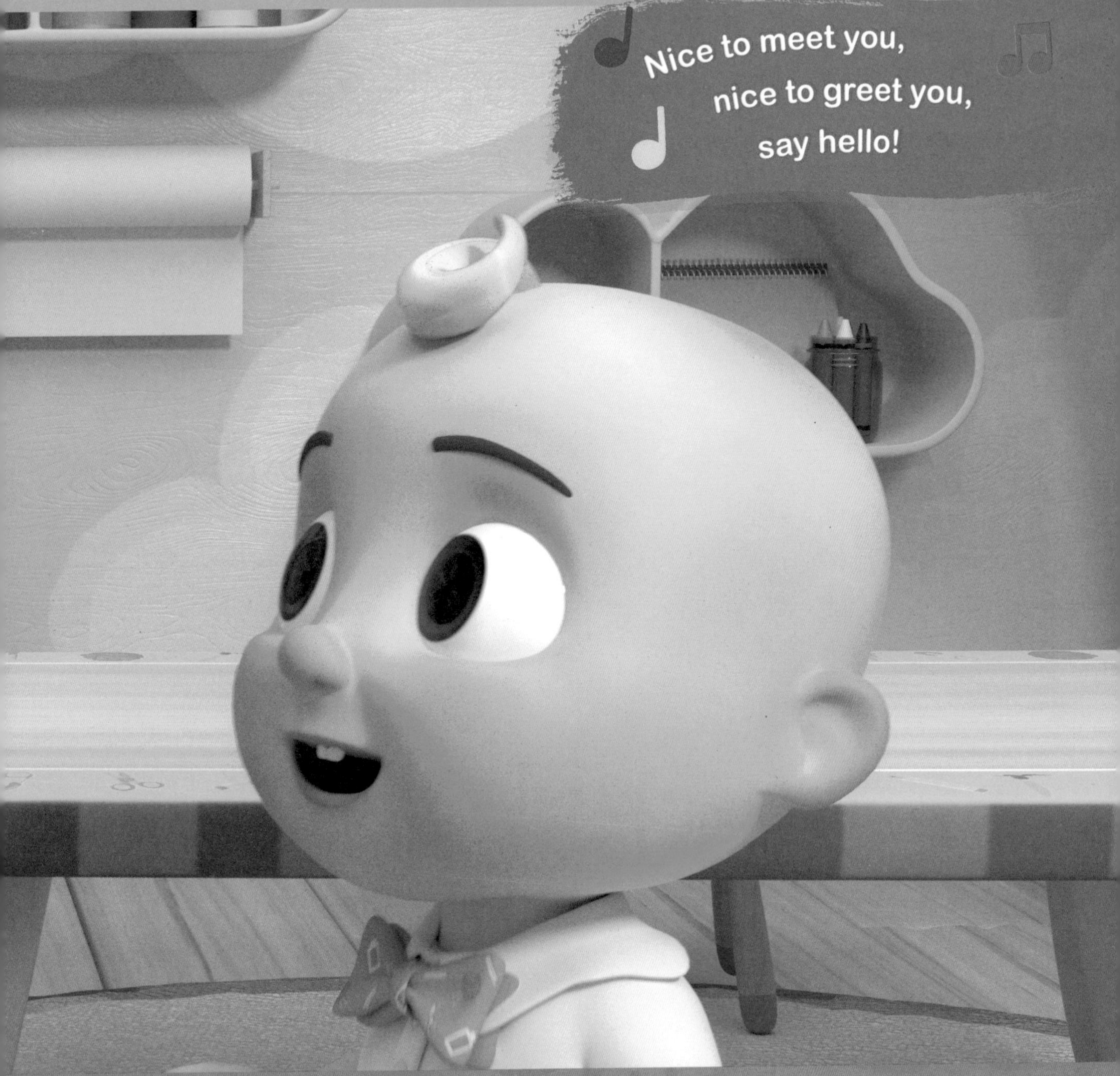

Nice to meet you,
nice to greet you,
say hello!

Hello, new friend!
Hello, new friend!
What's your name?

Hi! My name is Cody. JJ and I have lots of fun at school together. I love to play with toy dinosaurs.

And my name is Nina! JJ is one of my friends in my class. When I am at school, I love playing with stuffed bunnies. They are so soft and cuddly. *Hippity-hop!*

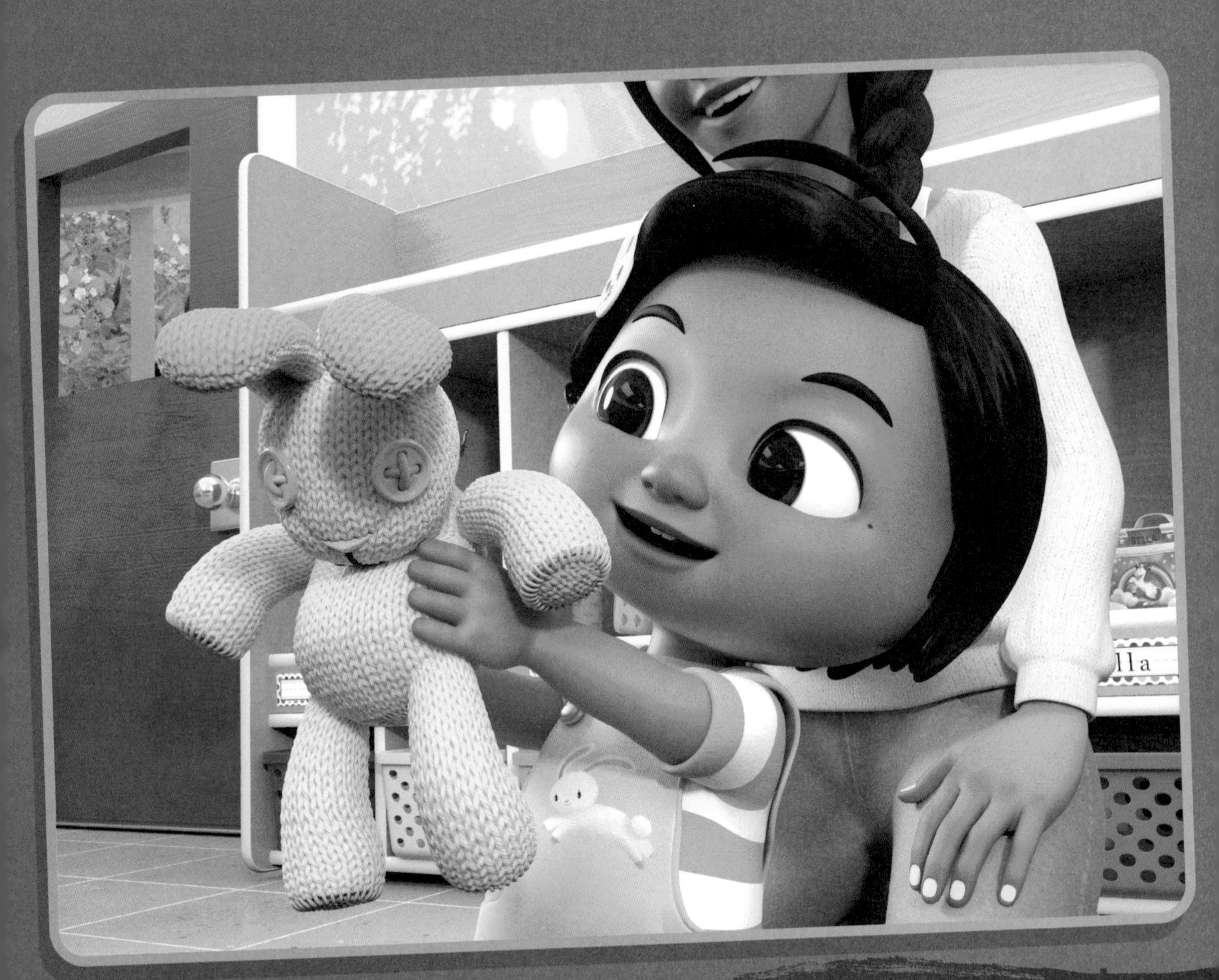

Nice to meet you,
nice to greet you,
say hello!

Hello! My name is Cece. JJ is one of my friends at school too! When I am at school, I love playing with my pink stuffed kitten. *Meowwww!*

Hello, new friend!
Hello, new friend!
What's your name?

Hi, everyone! My name is Ms. Appleberry. I love reading books, but I love teaching my students most of all!

Hello, new friend! Hello, new friend!
What's your name,
and what do you like?

Nice to meet you,
nice to greet you,
say hello!

READY FOR SCHOOL!

JJ is getting ready for school tomorrow, and his family wants to help him choose the right things to bring.

Tomorrow I am going to my school!

I can't wait to go to my school!

YoYo, JJ's sister, walks by with her polka-dot backpack.

"I need a backpack!" JJ says.

What do I need to bring
to my school?

TomTom, JJ's brother, puts a sticker with JJ's name on a shark backpack.

JJ loves it! He gives TomTom a big hug to thank him.

What else do I need to bring to my school?

JJ holds up his yellow ball.

"Hmm," his daddy says, shaking his head no.

"Do I need a water bottle?" JJ asks. His daddy gives him a thumbs-up!

"Can I bring ice cream?" JJ asks.
"Hmm," his mommy says, shaking her head no.
Ice Cream
What else do I need to
bring to my school?

JJ watches his mommy pack his lunch, and he remembers something else he needs. “I need my lunch box!” he says.

This time, his mommy smiles and nods.

The next morning, JJ is getting dressed to go to school. "Do I need my jacket?" he asks. "And my shoes, too?"

"Yes!" YoYo says.

I'm all ready! I'm all ready!
I'm all ready to go to my school.

JJ arrives at school. He gives his mommy a big hug before going off to join his friends.

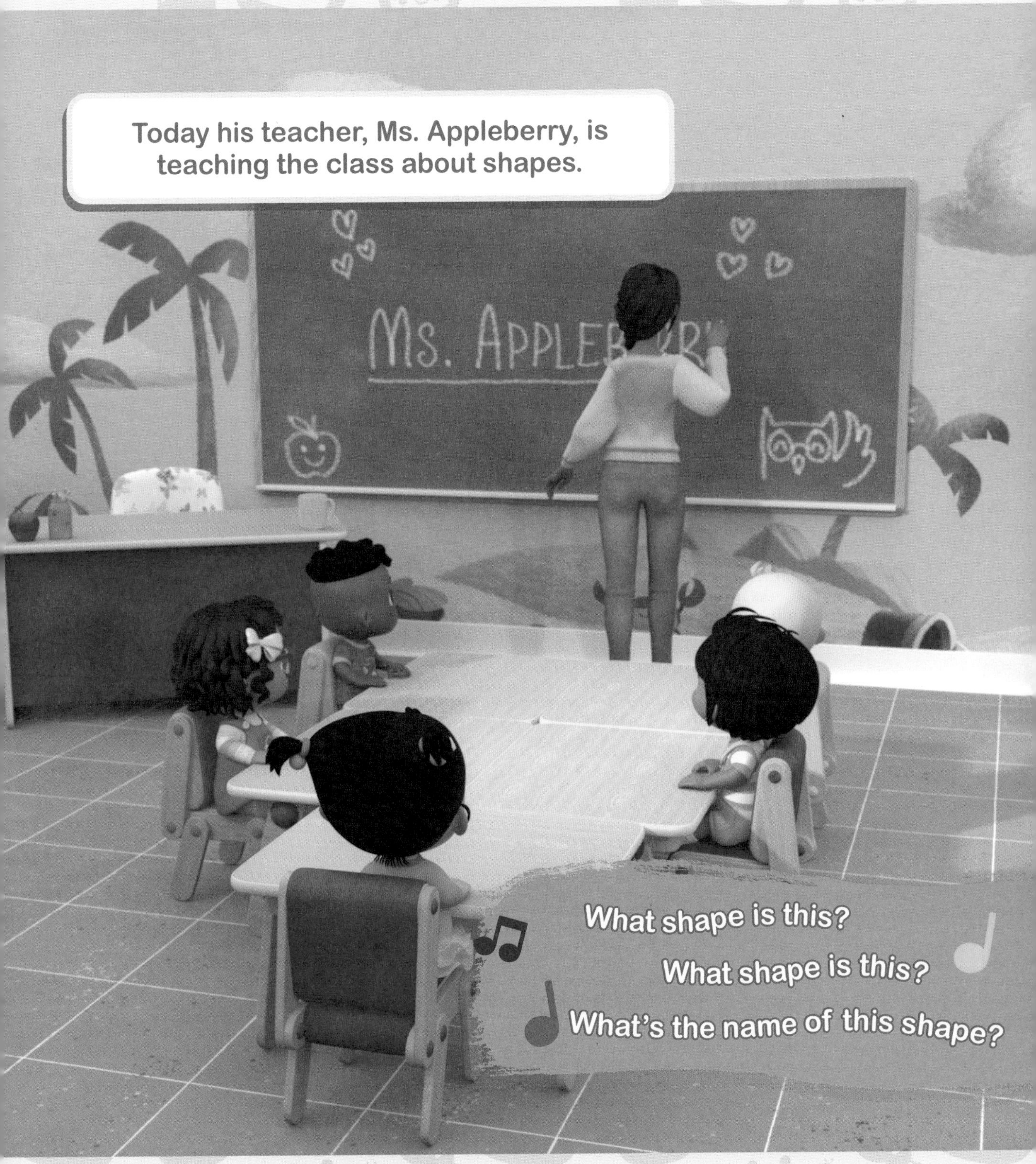

Today his teacher, Ms. Appleberry, is teaching the class about shapes.

What shape is this?

What shape is this?

What's the name of this shape?

It's got four sides.
It's got four corners.
What's the name of this shape?
"It's a rectangle!" says Cody.
"What thing can you think of that is a rectangle?" Ms. Appleberry asks.
A cubby!

It's got no sides.
It's got no corners.
What's the name of this shape?

"It's a circle!" says Bella.

"What thing can you think of that is a circle?" Ms. Appleberry asks. Balloons!

It's got three sides.
It's got three corners.
What's the name of this shape?

"It's a triangle," says JJ.
"Just like my party hat!"

"Great job!" says Ms. Appleberry.

Now it is time to eat lunch.
Ms. Appleberry points out the different colors in everyone's lunches.

Colors are so wonderful,
shining bright and beautiful!

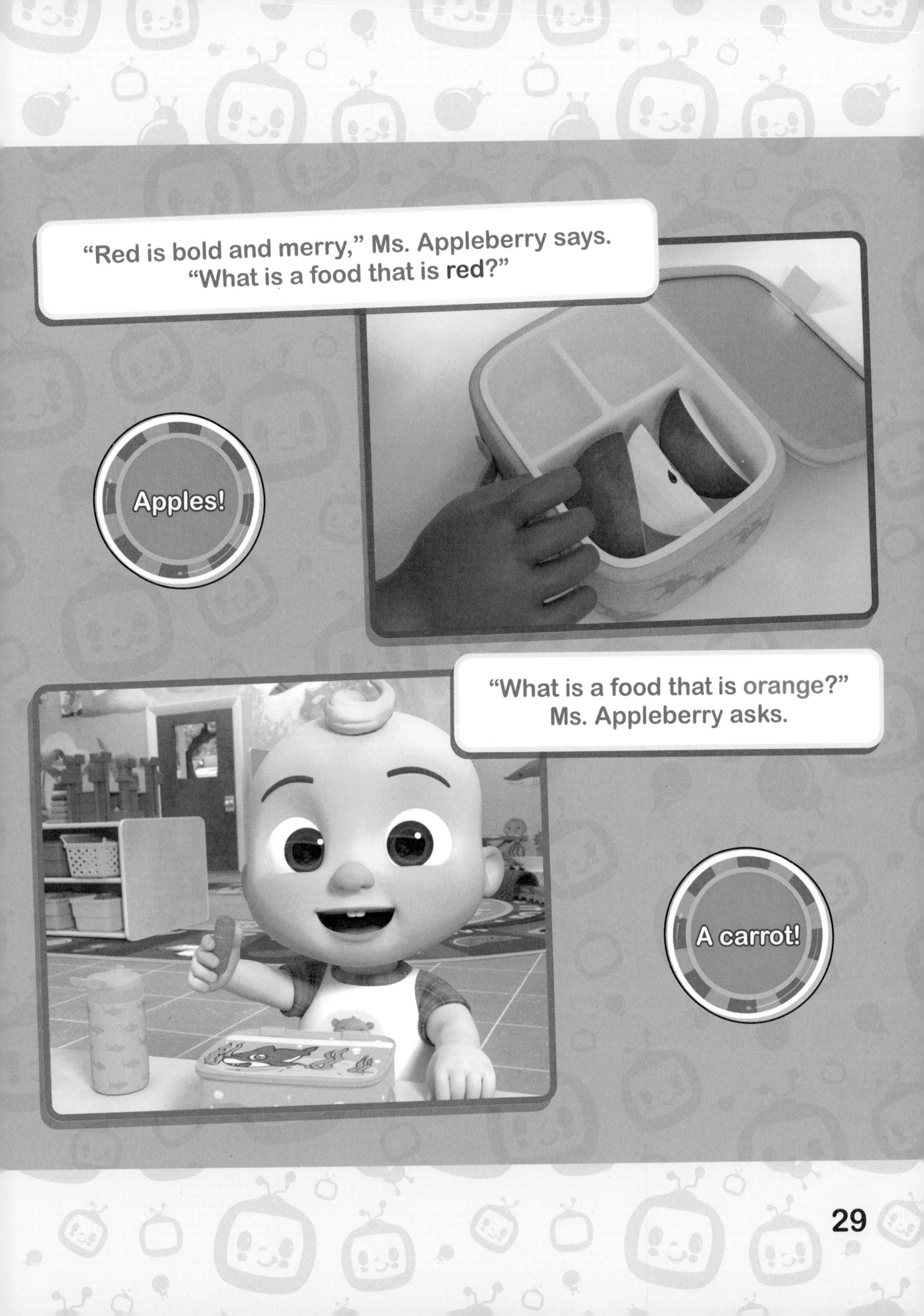
"Red is bold and merry," Ms. Appleberry says.
"What is a food that is red?"
Apples!
"What is a food that is orange?"
Ms. Appleberry asks.
A carrot!

"Blue is cool and calm," Ms. Appleberry says. "What is a food that is **blue**?"
Blueberry muffins!
"What about **purple**?" Ms. Appleberry asks.
Grape juice!

After lunch, it's time to take a nap. JJ and his friends lie down on their mats.

Let's all count sheep.
Count 1, 2, 3.
Until we sleep, let's all count sheep.

When nap time is done,
time to have more fun!

JJ colors a picture with crayons. The whale is white and blue, just like his shirt!

The classroom door opens. JJ's mommy is here to pick him up! "Did you have fun today?" she asks.
"Yes, I did!" JJ answers.
JJ waves goodbye to Ms. Appleberry and all his friends. He can't wait to return to school tomorrow!

LET'S MEET THE DOCTOR!

Today Cody's mom is visiting his school. She is a doctor!

She is going to explain to the class what happens when you go to see your doctor for a checkup!

When you go see the doctor
for your checkup today,
they will make sure you're healthy
in every way!

First they will check your weight to make sure you are growing strong and healthy.

Next they will check your height to see how many inches you have grown!

When you go see the doctor
for your checkup today,
they will make sure you're healthy
in every way!

The doctor will also check your lungs and heart by using a stethoscope. This helps the doctor hear your heartbeat and listen to your breathing.

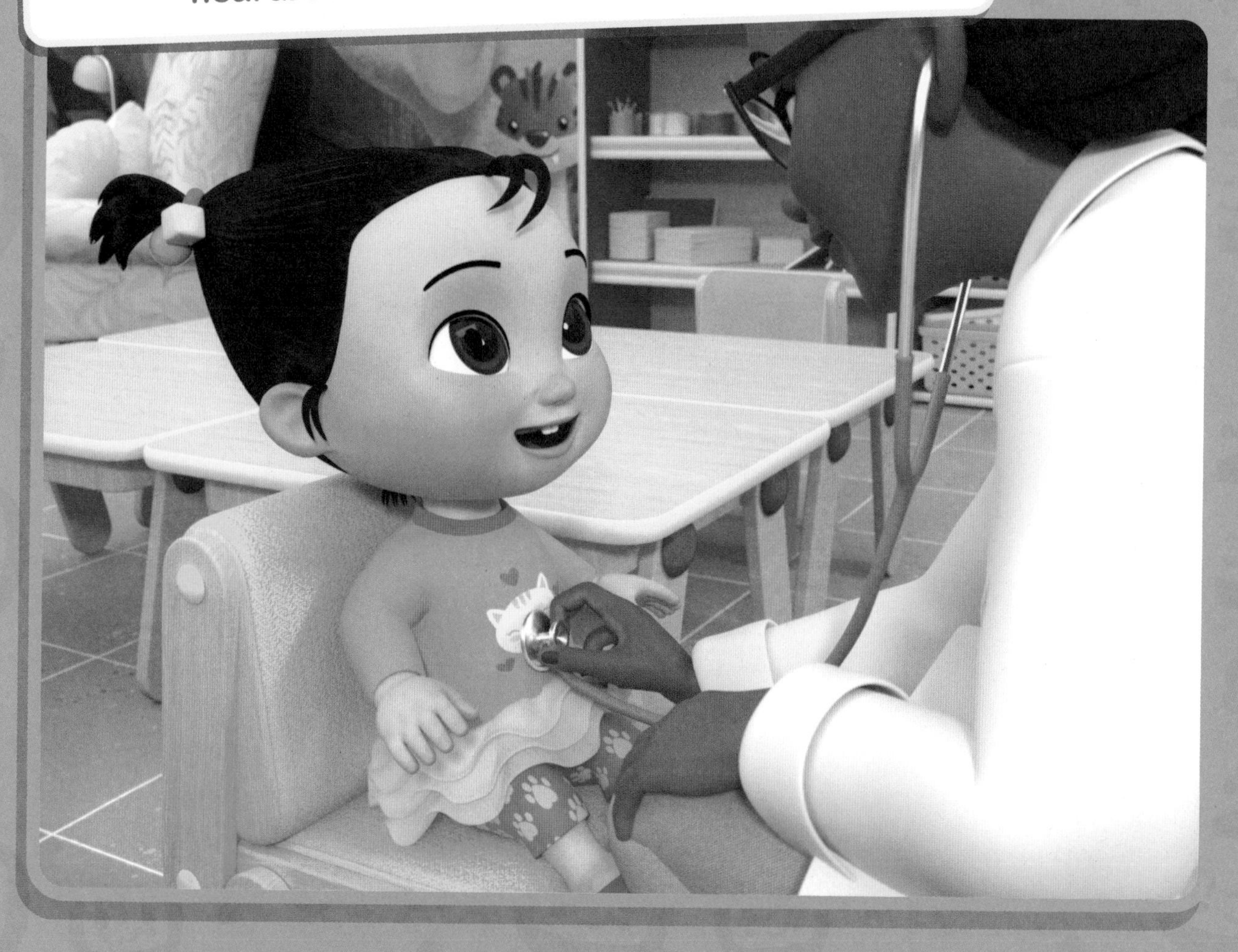

The doctor will also check your ears to make sure your hearing is A-OK!

Then the doctor will check your eyes by having you read an eye chart.

When you go see the doctor
for your checkup today,
they will make sure you're healthy
in every way!

The doctor will check your mouth and throat to make sure everything looks healthy. Say "AHHHH!"

The doctor will check your reflexes by tapping your knee with a rubber hammer.

But don't worry! It doesn't hurt—it tickles!

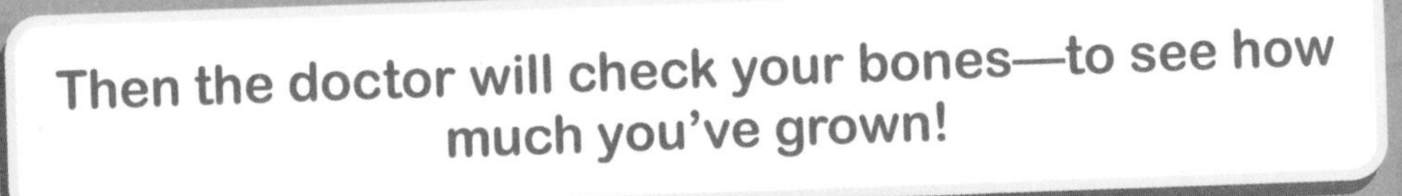
Then the doctor will check your bones—to see how much you've grown!

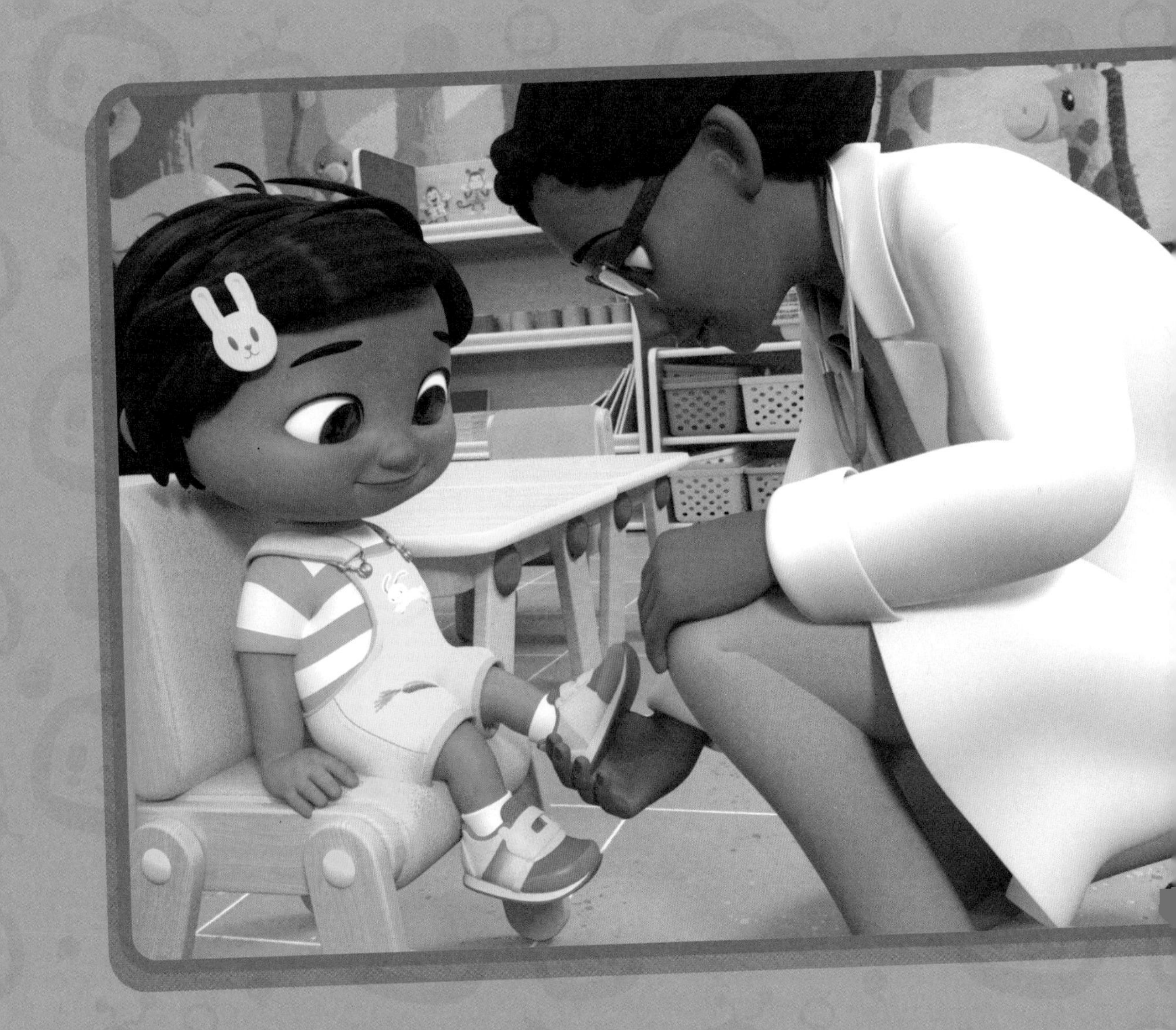

The doctor might say that you need a shot. But don't worry—it doesn't hurt a lot!

After your checkup is over, guess what? You might even get a special treat, like a sticker!

Bye, Doctor! Thanks for visiting!
When you go see the doctor
for your checkup today,
they will make sure you're healthy
in every way!

THE WHEELS ON THE BUS

JJ's class is going on a field trip to a museum! They get on the bus and buckle up. It's time to go for a ride!

What does JJ do on the bus? Sing a song, of course!
All his friends sing along with him too.

The wheels on the bus go round and round,
round and round, round and round.
The wheels on the bus go round and round
all through the town.

It starts to rain, but inside the bus, it's still warm and dry.

The wipers on the bus go swish, swish, swish,
swish, swish, swish, swish, swish, swish.
The wipers on the bus go swish, swish, swish
all through the town.

Then the bus makes a turn at the next stop sign.

The signals on the bus go blink, blink, blink,
blink, blink, blink, blink, blink, blink.
The signals on the bus go blink, blink, blink
all through the town.

The rain stops, and the sun comes out. "Hooray!" JJ cheers. He's feeling extra lucky today. Maybe a rainbow will appear! Then the bus driver honks the horn. . . .

The horn on the bus goes beep, beep, beep,
beep, beep, beep, beep, beep, beep.
The horn on the bus goes beep, beep, beep
all through the town.

The motor on the bus goes vroom, vroom, vroom,
vroom, vroom, vroom, vroom, vroom, vroom.
The motor on the bus goes vroom, vroom, vroom
all through the town.

The bus comes to a stop at the museum, and the driver turns around. He says to JJ and the other kids, "I have a song to sing. . . ."

The wheels on the bus go round and round,
round and round, round and round.
The wheels on the bus go round and round . . .
and now we're here!

YES, YES, VEGETABLES!

PEAS! PEAS!

It's time to eat your peas!
Yes, yes, yes, I want to eat my peas!
Good, good! The peas are good for you!
Yay, yay, yay, I love them, oooh!

JJ and Teddy love to eat peas.
Do you like to eat your peas?

I like them, wow!

CARROTS! CARROTS!

It's time to eat your carrots!
Yes, yes, yes, I want to eat my carrots!
Good, good! The carrots are good for you!
Yay, yay, yay, I love them, oooh!

JJ and Elephant love to eat carrots.
Do you like to eat your carrots?

I like them, wow!

SQUASH! SQUASH!

It's time to eat your squash!
Yes, yes, yes, I want to eat my squash!
Good, good! The squash is good for you!
Yay, yay, yay, I love them, oooh!

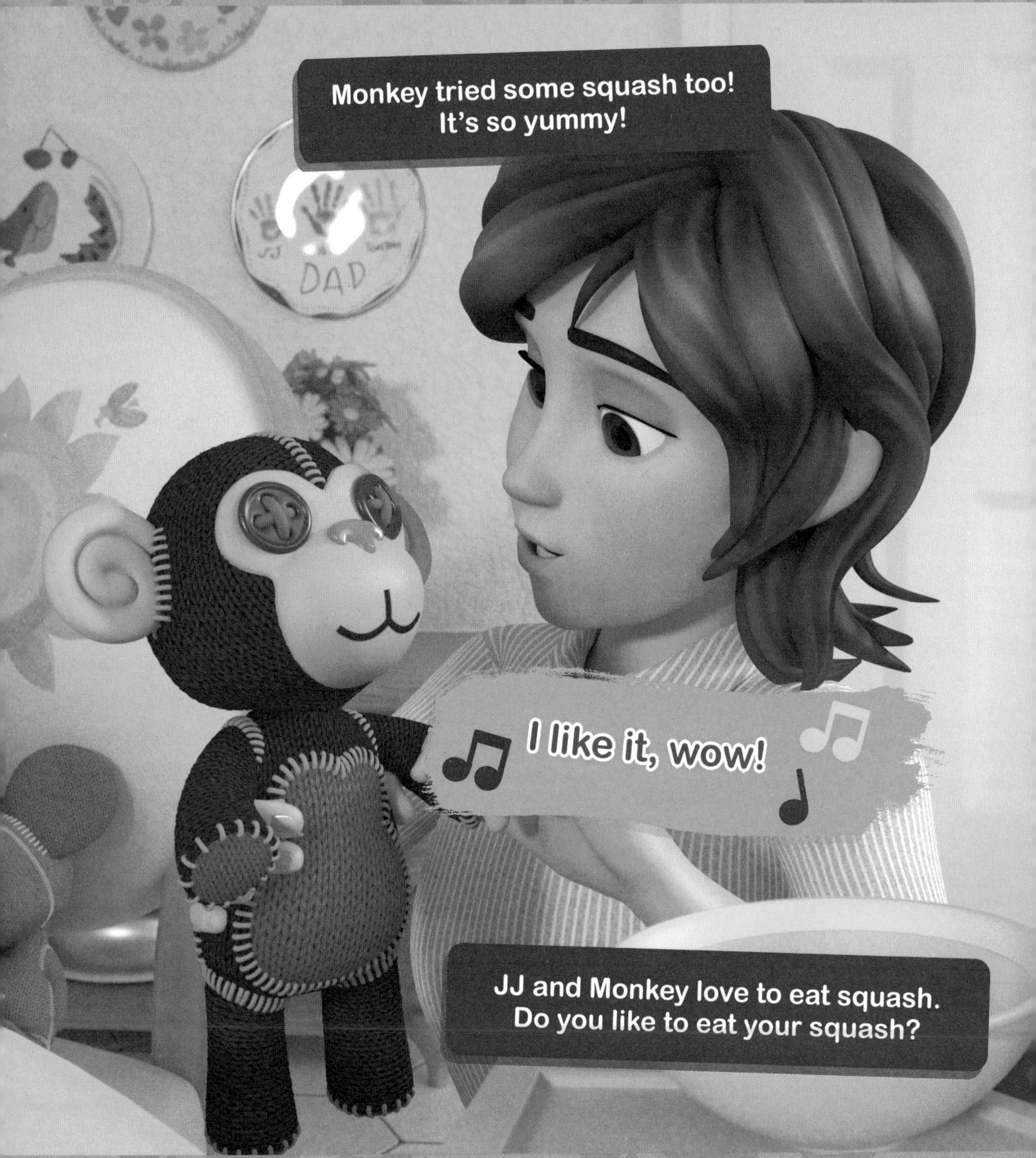

Monkey tried some squash too!
It's so yummy!

I like it, wow!

JJ and Monkey love to eat squash.
Do you like to eat your squash?

BEANS! BEANS!

It's time to eat your beans!
Yes, yes, yes, I want to eat my beans!
Good, good! The beans are good for you!
Yay, yay, yay, I love them, oooh!

JJ and Mousie love to eat beans.
Do you like to eat your beans?

I like them, wow!

BROCCOLI! BROCCOLI!

It's time to eat your broccoli!
Yes, yes, yes, I want to eat my broccoli!
Good, good! The broccoli is good for you!
Yay, yay, yay, I love them, oooh!

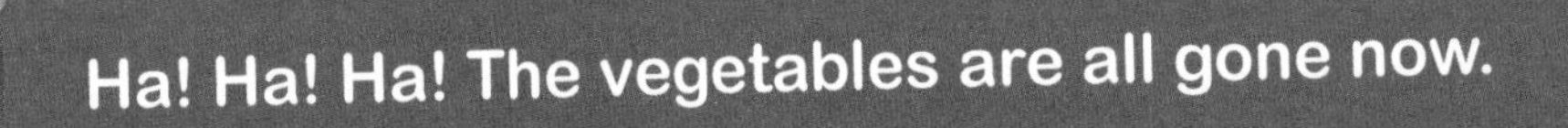

Yum! Yum! Yum!
We like them, wow!

High five! What are some of your favorite vegetables?

SWEET, SWEET BEDTIME

The sun is setting outside. It's time to get ready for bed!

First JJ is going to brush his teeth. Mommy gives the toothpaste tube a big squeeze. JJ brushes his teeth left to right. The toothpaste makes a lot of bubbles inside JJ's mouth!

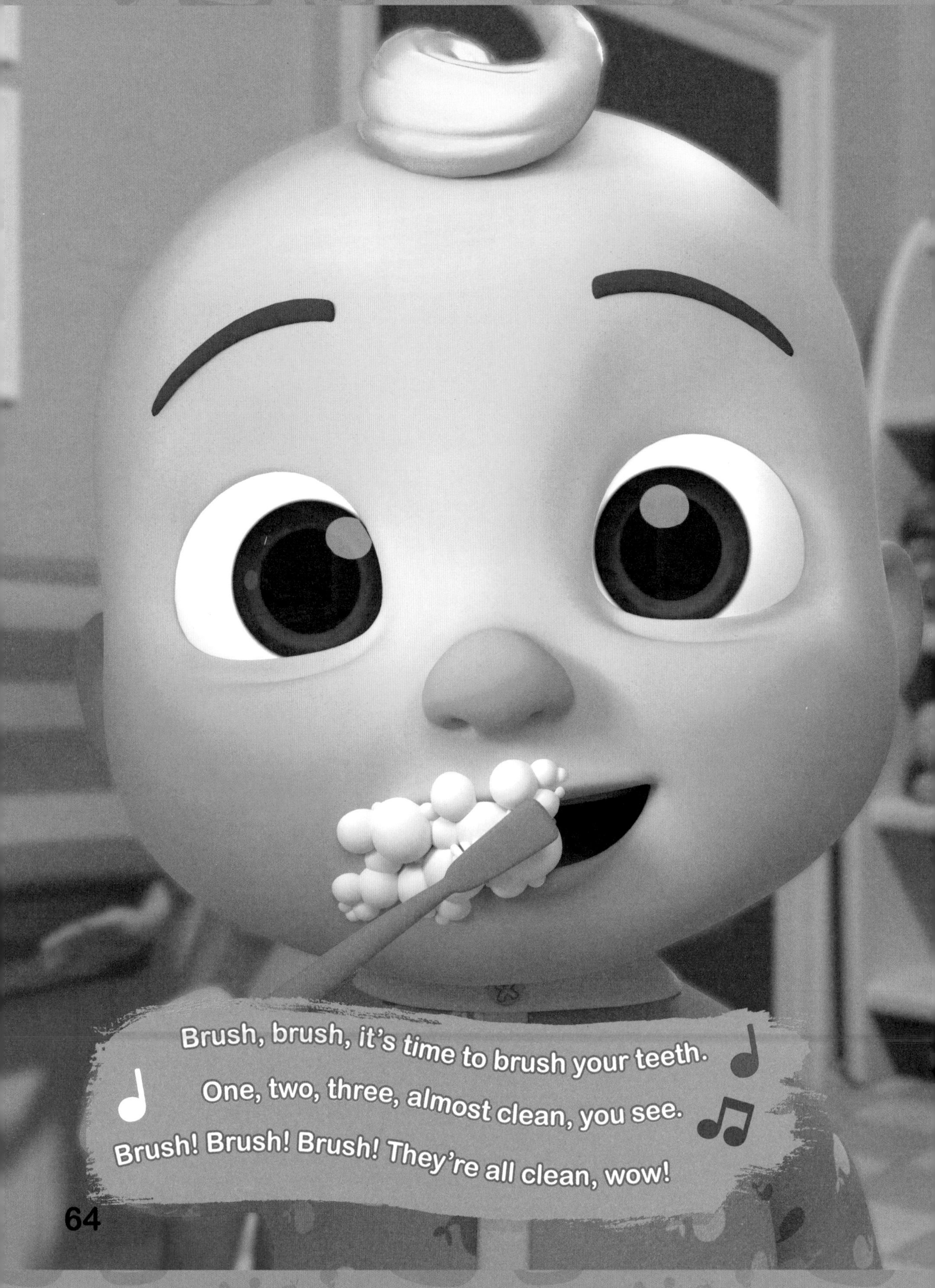

Brush, brush, it's time to brush your teeth.
One, two, three, almost clean, you see.
Brush! Brush! Brush! They're all clean, wow!

Now it's time for JJ to take a bath. Mommy pours JJ's favorite bubbles into the tub. JJ loves splashing in the warm water!

Bath, bath, it's time to take a bath.
One, two, three, almost clean, you see.
Splash! Splash! Splash! We like it, wow!

JJ dries off with a towel and goes to his bedroom. Now it's time to put on some soft pajamas! They're his favorite color: blue!

Pajamas, pajamas, it's time to wear pajamas.
One, two, three, almost on, you see.
Soft! Soft! Soft! We like them, wow!

Mommy helps JJ get into bed. Teddy will keep him company during the night! JJ feels warm and happy snuggling Teddy.

Bed, bed, it's time to get in bed.
One, two, three, cozy warm, you see.
Cozy! Cozy! Cozy! We like it, wow!

Now it is story time. Mommy reads a counting book to help JJ fall asleep.

Story, story, it's time to read a story.
One, two, three, almost done, you see.
Fun! Fun! Fun! We like it, wow!

Mommy gives JJ a good-night kiss and tucks him into bed.

HAVE A SWEET, SWEET BEDTIME!

COCOMELON ABCs

JJ is playing a game with his sister, YoYo, and his brother, TomTom! They're looking for objects around the house that start with different letters of the alphabet. Come along and help them find all twenty-six letters!

An apple starts with A.

Book starts with B.

JJ loves it when
his siblings read to him
before bedtime!

C is for cake . . .
with cherries on top!
D is for Daddy.
E is for eggs of
every shape.

Can you find anything in YoYo's room that starts with the letter F?

"I see flowers and a fence!" says YoYo.

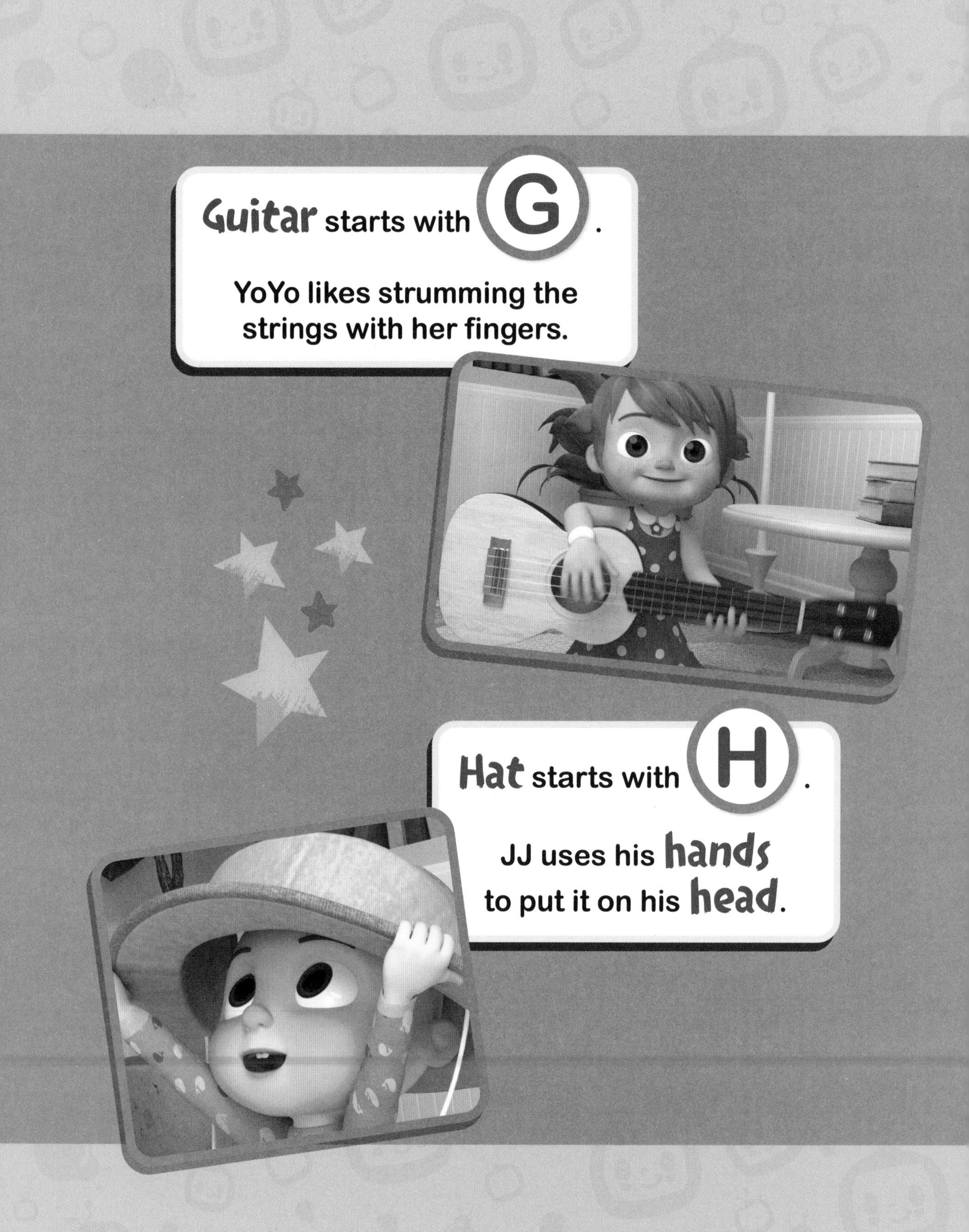

Guitar starts with **G**.

YoYo likes strumming the strings with her fingers.

Hat starts with **H**.

JJ uses his **hands** to put it on his **head**.

JJ, YoYo, and TomTom go to the kitchen to find things that start with I.

Look! TomTom has made a little igloo out of ice cubes. Incredible!

YoYo has a glass of juice, which starts with a J. She gives it to JJ.

Kitchen starts with **K**.

TomTom finds **kiwis**
in the fridge.

L is for a **lemon** so sour, it makes YoYo's **lips** pucker up!

M is for **Mommy**.

"My **mouth** starts with **M** too!" Mommy says.

Nose and neck both start with N.

Orange is an object that starts with O.

What objects in the living room start with P ?
That's right!
Piano, plant, and picture!

YoYo puts a crown on her head.

"Queen starts with Q!" she says.

The ring on her finger starts with R.

SPACE CADET CLIFF
BASEBALL
TomTom's room has stars and a space shuttle painted on the walls.
They both start with S!

JJ has two friends whose names start with T.

They are Teddy and TomTom!

U is for umbrella.
TomTom uses one on rainy days to stay dry.
Vegetables start with V.
They are very, very yummy!

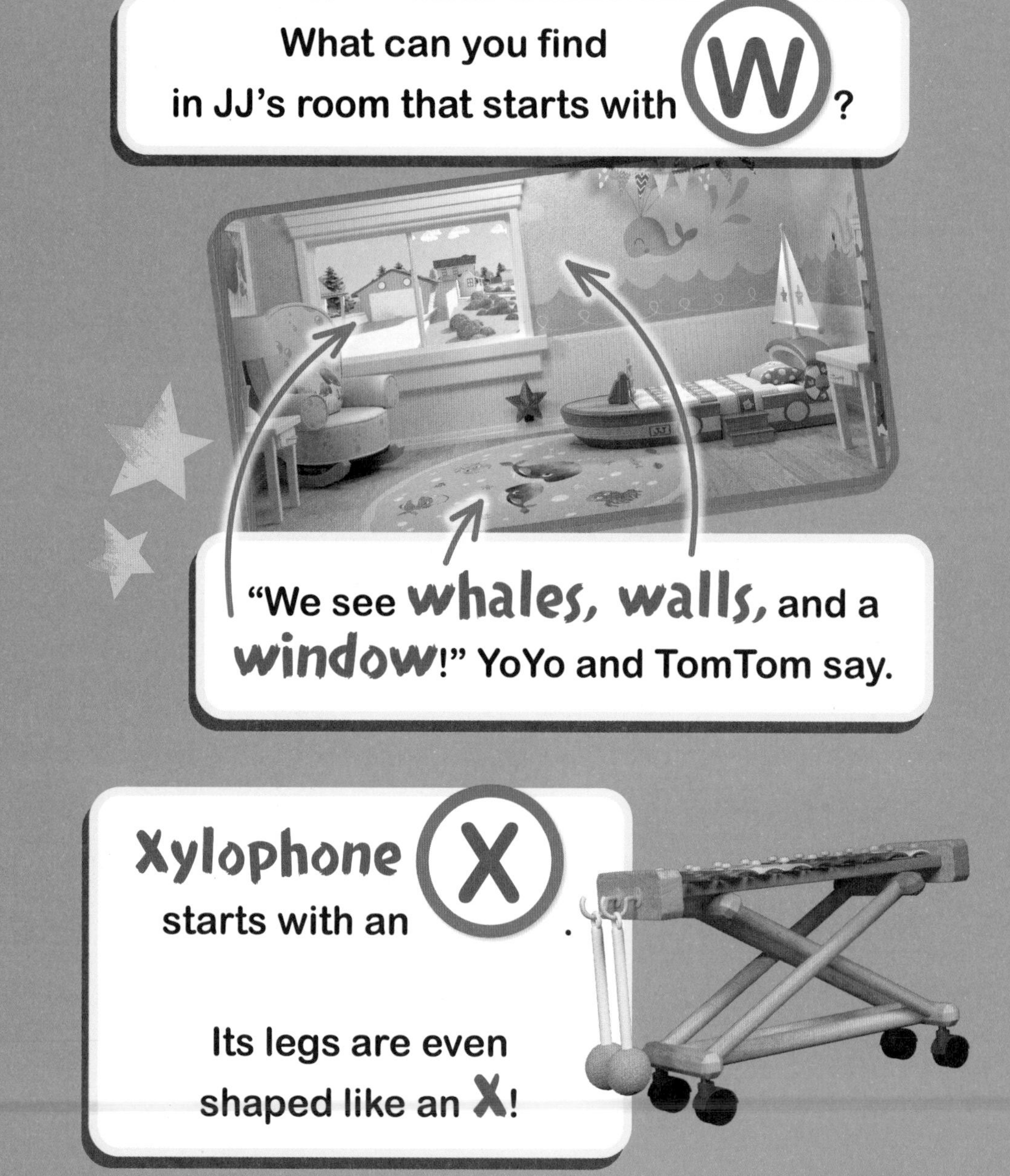

What can you find in JJ's room that starts with W?

"We see **whales, walls,** and a **window**!" YoYo and TomTom say.

Xylophone starts with an X.

Its legs are even shaped like an **X**!

Y is for YoYo.

Does YoYo like playing with a toy yo-yo?
"You bet!" she says.

Now they only have one letter left to find . . . and JJ finds it on his jacket!

Zipper starts with Z!

Thank you for helping JJ, YoYo, and TomTom find all the letters in the alphabet!

A B C D E F G
O P Q R S T

H I J K L M N

U V W X Y Z

Now I know my ABCs.
Next time won't you sing with me?

WHAT MAKES ME HAPPY

It is nighttime, and JJ is asleep.

Suddenly, there is a flash of light and a loud crash from outside the window.

JJ wakes up. He is scared and doesn't want to be alone.

When you're scared or feeling blue,
there is something you can do!

JJ crawls out of bed. He already feels much better when he sees his brother and sister in the hallway.

YoYo gives JJ a hug. “The storm scared me too,” she says.

TomTom has an idea. “I know where we can go,” he says, and YoYo and JJ follow him. “We will always be safe with Mommy and Daddy!”

There’s a place that you can go
that is always filled with joy.

JJ, YoYo, and TomTom listen carefully. Mommy and Daddy always know how to make them feel better.

"Do you know what makes me happy when I'm scared?" Mommy asks.

JJ shakes his head. "What makes you happy, Mommy?"

Mommy smiles. "It makes me happy to think of how much I love you," she says.

I look around and then I see many faces that make me feel happy.

What makes you happy?

TomTom is starting to feel better. "What makes you happy, Daddy?" he asks.

"It makes me happy when I see you smile. Can you think of what makes you happy?" Daddy asks.

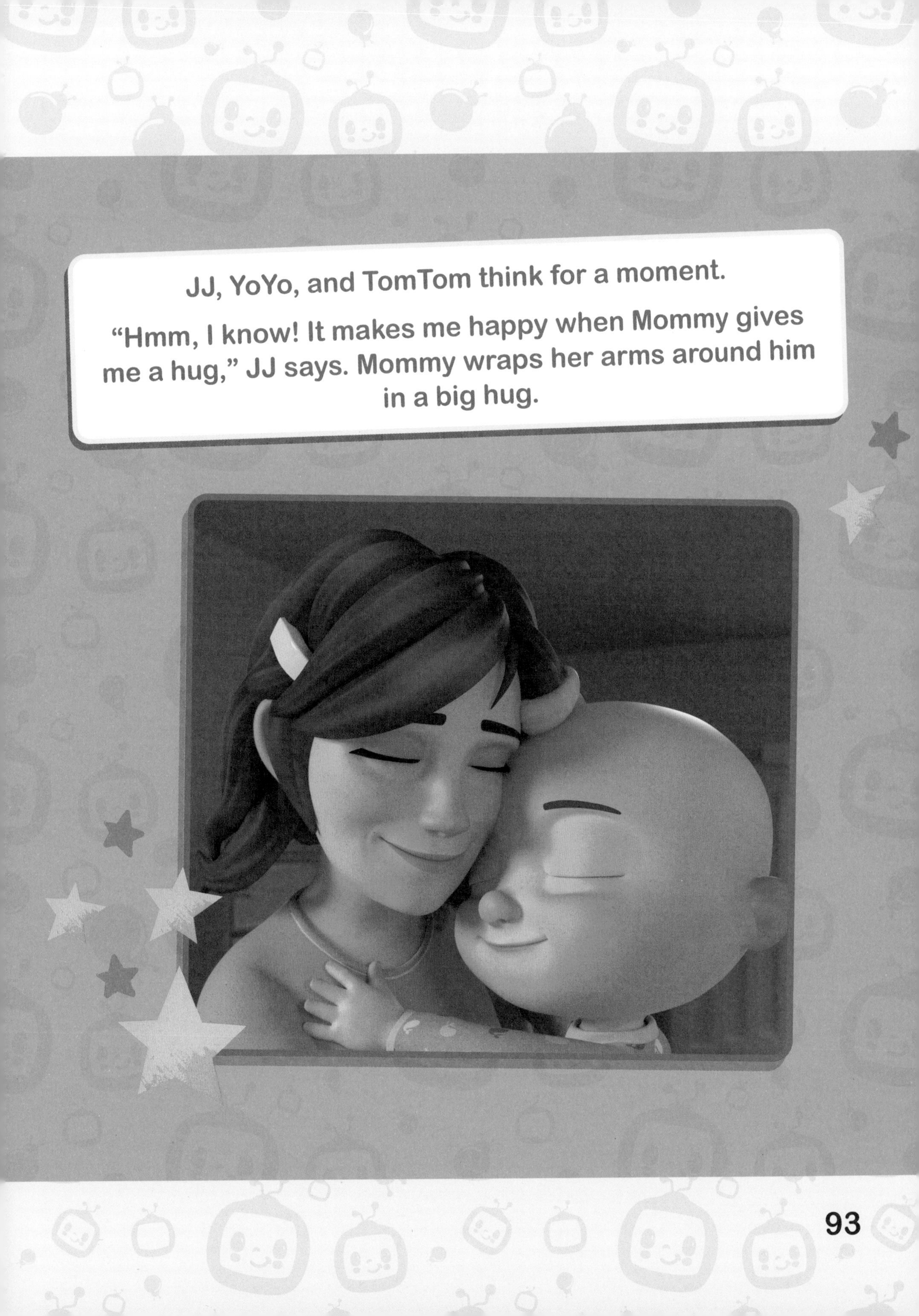

JJ, YoYo, and TomTom think for a moment.

"Hmm, I know! It makes me happy when Mommy gives me a hug," JJ says. Mommy wraps her arms around him in a big hug.

"Yes, Mommy's hugs are the best!" YoYo says.

"How about you, YoYo? What makes you happy?" Mommy asks.

YoYo thinks hard. She looks around and sees a picture of their grandpa. "Oh! Grandpa makes me happy when he comes to play!" she says.

"Can you think of what makes you happy, TomTom?" Daddy asks.

TomTom sees their dog, Bingo, rolling around on the floor, and he giggles. "Bingo makes me happy when he rolls around!" he says.

Mommy gives them a warm hug. “Thunder can be scary, but it will be okay,” she says.

It's right here, in your heart.
Always safe and never far.

JJ, YoYo, and TomTom like thinking about things that make them happy, but then they hear more thunder outside!

"Close your eyes, take a deep breath, and think about things that make you feel safe and happy," Daddy says.

"I'm scared, but I will be okay!" YoYo says with a brave smile.

TomTom nods and says, "We can think of things that make us happy."

TomTom has an idea. “I know! Let’s make a blanket fort.”

JJ nods with excitement. “Yes! Let’s make a bed of pillows inside!”

“We can hang stars inside too!” YoYo says.

What makes you happy?

JJ, YoYo, and TomTom feel so safe and happy inside their blanket fort.

JJ is surprised by another flash of lightning and a clap of thunder.

This time, YoYo and TomTom are not scared.

YoYo holds JJ's hand. "Close your eyes and take a deep breath," she says.

Look around and you will see lots of things that make you feel happy.

"Look around and think about what makes you happy," says TomTom.

“My teddy bear!” JJ says, and he gives his teddy bear a big hug.

“Can you remember what makes you feel happy?” YoYo asks.

What makes you happy?

Daddy makes them a cup of hot cocoa, and Mommy gives them each a kiss good night.

JJ, YoYo, and TomTom feel much better. The storm outside doesn't scare them anymore!

They will always remember things that make them happy.

The moments like this,
they make me happy.

JJ, YoYo, and TomTom fall asleep in the safety of their blanket fort and dream about things that make them happy.

There's a place that you can go
that is always filled with joy.

I'M A FIREFIGHTER!
JJ and his friends have a special visitor at school today. Who could it be? JJ can't wait to find out!

Nina's mom is a firefighter.
A big and brave firefighter!

A firefighter's job is to put out fires.
They help rescue people in danger.

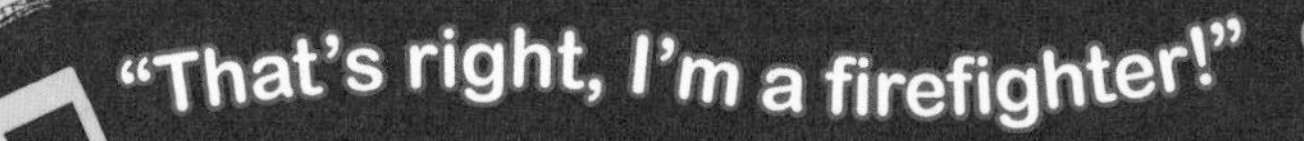

Nina's mom is here to teach JJ and his friends about staying safe in case of a fire at their school. Firefighters are important helpers!

Nina runs over to give her mom a hug and sings,

"I'm going to be a firefighter!"

Let's wear a bright red fire hat,
a shiny bright red fire hat.

Nina's mom wears a red fire hat that protects her head while she works. She wears the hat every day, just like JJ wears his helmet every time he rides his tricycle or scooter.

In a bright red fire hat,
I look like a firefighter.
Wee-ooh! Wee-ooh!

JJ and Nina think fire hats look bright and fun.

Let's wear a yellow fire coat,
a big and yellow fire coat.

Nina's mom also wears a fire coat. It's made from special materials, so her coat won't burn easily, even if flames touch it.

The coat also has bright stripes. The stripes help people see firefighters through smoke during a fire, and they also help people driving cars at night see firefighters on the road.

"Look at me!" Cody says, trying on a pretend fire coat.

Ms. Appleberry pulls out a pretend fire engine. It has a lot of wheels, and white ladders to reach tall places.

Let's get in the fire engine,
a big, red, shiny fire engine.

Nico and Bella get in the fire engine and pretend to ride around. "Fire engine coming through! Keep the streets clear!" Bella says.

In a big red fire engine,
I look like a firefighter.
Wee-ooh! Wee-ooh!

Nina's mom places a pretend fire in the corner of the classroom. "Oh no, there's a fire!" she says.

What will JJ and his friends do?

Let's use the whooshing water hose,
a whooshing, wiggling
water hose.

Water hoses are very long so they can reach almost anywhere . . . even tall buildings! Everyone works together to bring the hose closer to the imaginary fire.

With a whooshing water hose,
I look like a firefighter.
Wee-ooh! Wee-ooh!

Whooooosh!

Nina aims the hose at the imaginary flames, and the fire stops burning.

"Great job!" says Nina's mom. "Now, listen to Ms. Appleberry. I'll be back soon."

In a drill, there is no real fire. JJ and his friends pretend that there is a fire so they will know what to do if there is ever a fire at school.

WHOOP!
WHOOP!
WHOOP!

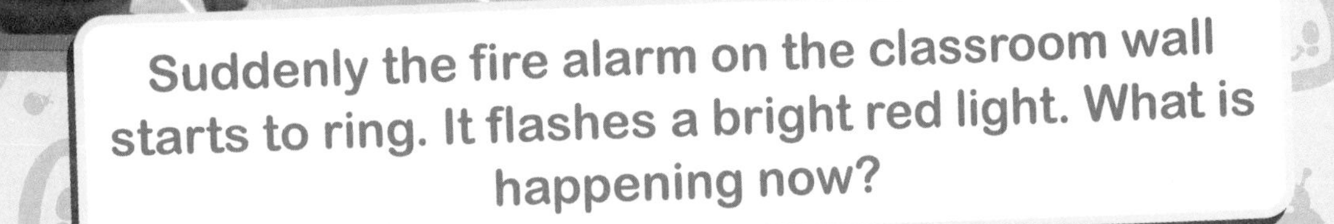

Suddenly the fire alarm on the classroom wall starts to ring. It flashes a bright red light. What is happening now?

Let's listen to the teacher now.
I'm listening to the teacher now.
Because the teacher is telling me now,
we are putting on a fire drill!

WHOOP!
WHOOP!
WHOOP!

JJ stays calm and listens to Ms. Appleberry's directions. "Line up and follow me outside," Ms. Appleberry says.

Let's line up safe and sound outside.
We'll gather in a line outside.

One by one, JJ and his friends leave the classroom and move away from the building.

Ms. Appleberry takes roll call to make sure everyone is in line and safe.

"JJ?" says Ms. Appleberry.

"Here!" says JJ.

"Nina?" says Ms. Appleberry.

"Here!" says Nina.

We'll be safe lined up outside.

We'll wait for the firefighter.

"Look!" Nina says, pointing. A big red fire engine, with its sirens blaring, parks in front of the school. Nina's mom hops out of the truck.

Wee-ooh! Wee-ooh!

Nina's mom looks to make sure there is no fire in the school. She also checks whether anyone is in danger.

"Everything looks good!" she says.

JJ feels safe, knowing that Ms. Appleberry and Nina's mom are here to help during a fire.

"When I grow up, I want to be a brave firefighter and help people, just like you do!" Nina says to her mom.

"You will be a great firefighter!" her mom says.

I LIKE MY NAME

"Hi!" says JJ. He is getting ready to go to school, where he can learn and play with his friends.

Nice to meet you!
Nice to meet you!

JJ likes his name. It starts with "J" and ends with "J" because there are two "J"s in it. JJ's name shares the same first letter as the name of his classroom's pet hamster: Jelly Bean! Sometimes Jelly Bean sleeps over at JJ's house.

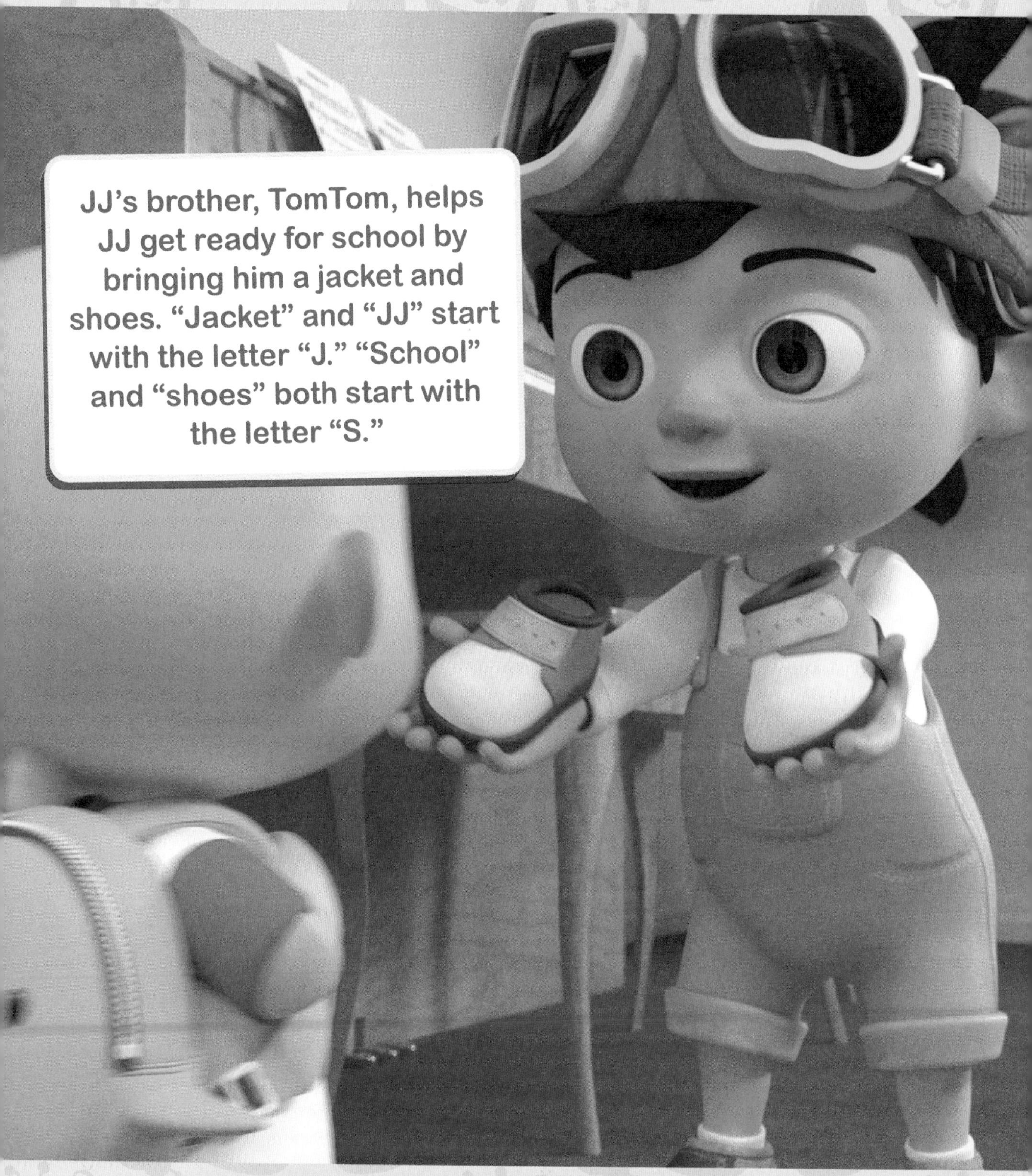

JJ’s brother, TomTom, helps JJ get ready for school by bringing him a jacket and shoes. “Jacket” and “JJ” start with the letter “J.” “School” and “shoes” both start with the letter “S.”

TomTom's name starts with the letter "T." What are some items around the house that also start with the letter "T"?
TEDDY
TUB
TRUCKS
TomTom waves to Teddy.
How do you do?
How do you do?

YoYo, JJ and TomTom's sister,
is also getting ready for school.
"Hello!" she says.

YoYo's name starts with the letter "Y." For today's breakfast, she's eating something that also begins with "Y": yogurt!

JJ, TomTom, and YoYo get on the yellow school bus to go to school. "Yellow" also starts with "Y."

The wheels on the bus go round and round, all through the town!

When JJ gets to school, his friends are excited to see him. Do you know this friend's name?

My name is . . . Cece!

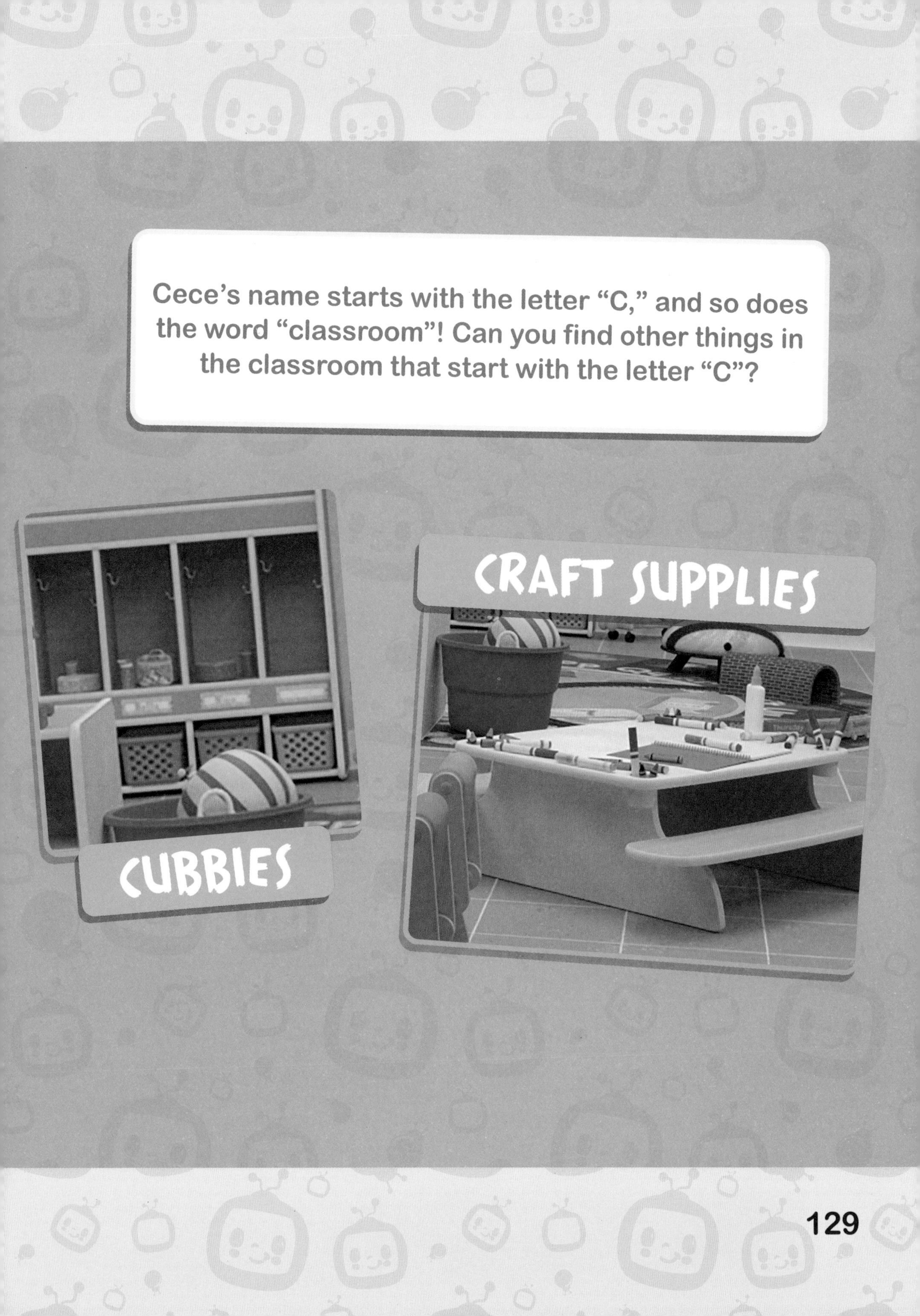
Cece's name starts with the letter "C," and so does the word "classroom"! Can you find other things in the classroom that start with the letter "C"?
CUBBIES
CRAFT SUPPLIES

Nina thinks Cece's name is fun and cheery, just like Cece herself.

"Thank you!" Cece says.

I like your name. Wow!
I like your name. Wow!

Nina's name starts with the letter "N" . . . just like the word "name"! Can you think of other words that start with "N"?

Bella wants to join the fun too.

"Your name starts with a 'B,'" Cece says to Bella. "Just like the bow in your hair!"

"'Bunny' starts with 'B' too!" Nina says. "That's my favorite animal."

Let's play together!
Let's all be friends!

Can you think of any more words that start with a "B" besides "Bella," "bow," and "bunny?"
BACKPACK
BUS
BALLOONS

Soon Cody and Nico arrive at school.

Cody's name starts with a "C," just like "Cece's." Nico's name starts with an "N," just like "Nina's."

"Good morning!" says JJ's teacher, Ms. Appleberry.

"Teacher" starts with the letter "T," just like the name of JJ's brother! Do you remember what JJ's brother's name is?

Now that everyone has arrived, it's time for school to begin!

CODY'S DINO DAY!

It's a special day, hooray!
My school has planned a Dino Day!

Cody and JJ pretend they are dinosaurs!
I want to roar!
I want to shout!

Suddenly JJ and Cody notice something on the bulletin board. It looks like Dino Day has been . . . canceled!

But Dino Day is not happening now . . .

"Hey, buddy," Cody's dad says. "Don't worry. You can make your own special day!"

Cody feels hopeful. He is going to try and make the most out of today!
He shows his friends his paper dinosaurs and asks them to play.

But they are too interested in the monkeys that Ms. Appleberry is showing them.

Cody is sad. This day doesn't feel very special at all.

My special day has gone away
now that it's not Dino Day.
Don't want to roar, just want to pout,
'cause Dino Day's not happening now.

Cody is so disappointed. He tries to have fun with his classmates, but he is not having a very good time at all.

Soon it's time for recess. But Cody doesn't feel like playing. He sits at a table alone.

Cody's dad stops by to check on Cody.

"What's wrong, buddy?"
Cody's dad asks him.

Cody looks down at his dinosaur toys sadly. “I just wanted today to be special,” Cody says quietly.

Cody's dad hands him a surprise. It's a special box filled with yummy treats like dinosaur cookies!

Cody's dad gives him some advice.

You can make your own happiness.
Give it a try. Take a look inside!

But Cody's dad wasn't talking about looking inside the box.

Take a look inside . . . your heart!
You can make your own happiness.

The day will be special—
just bring what's outside . . . inside!

"Yeah," Cody says. "I can make my own special Dino Day!"

Cody runs onto the playground and waves at his friends. JJ, Bella, and Cece are so happy that he wants to play again!

Come play with us, Cody!

PLAYDATE WITH CODY

JJ is so excited. His best friend, Cody, is coming over for a playdate!

"I can't wait to see JJ!"
Cody says.

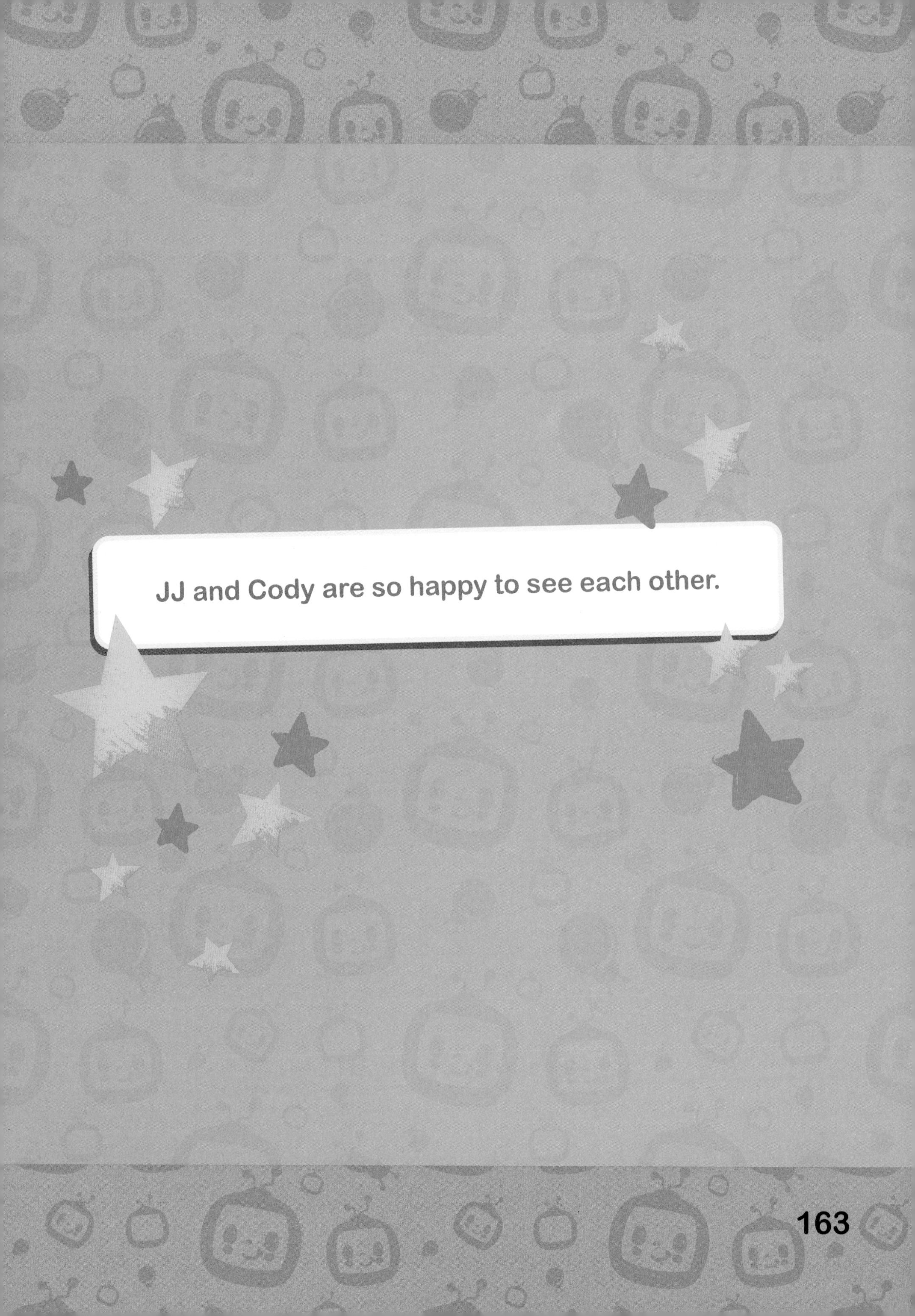
JJ and Cody are so happy to see each other.

Today's our day to play!

Having lots of fun!

Playing with my dinosaur!

Oh no! We just have one.

Their dads remind them, "When we work together, everyone has more fun!"
JJ

Cody chooses to share his dinosaur with JJ.

It's better to work together
because it's double the fun!

I have fun when you have fun! Yes!
Share when you only have one!

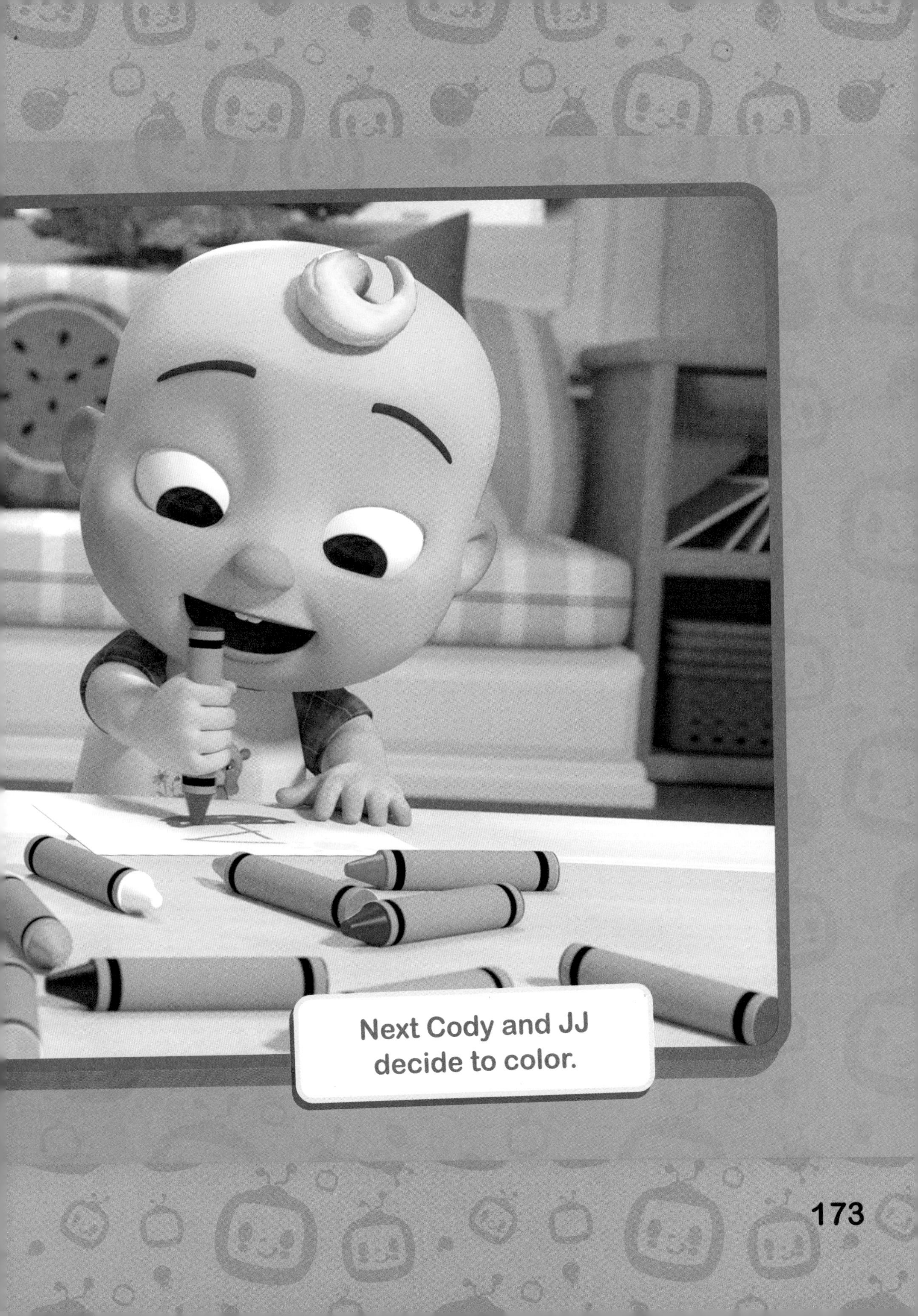

Next Cody and JJ
decide to color.

Oh no! Cody and JJ both want
the same dark blue crayon.

I want the color blue.
Oh no! We just have one.

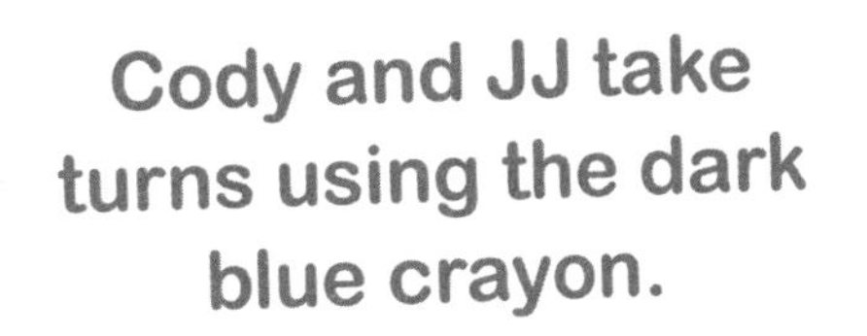
Cody and JJ take turns using the dark blue crayon.

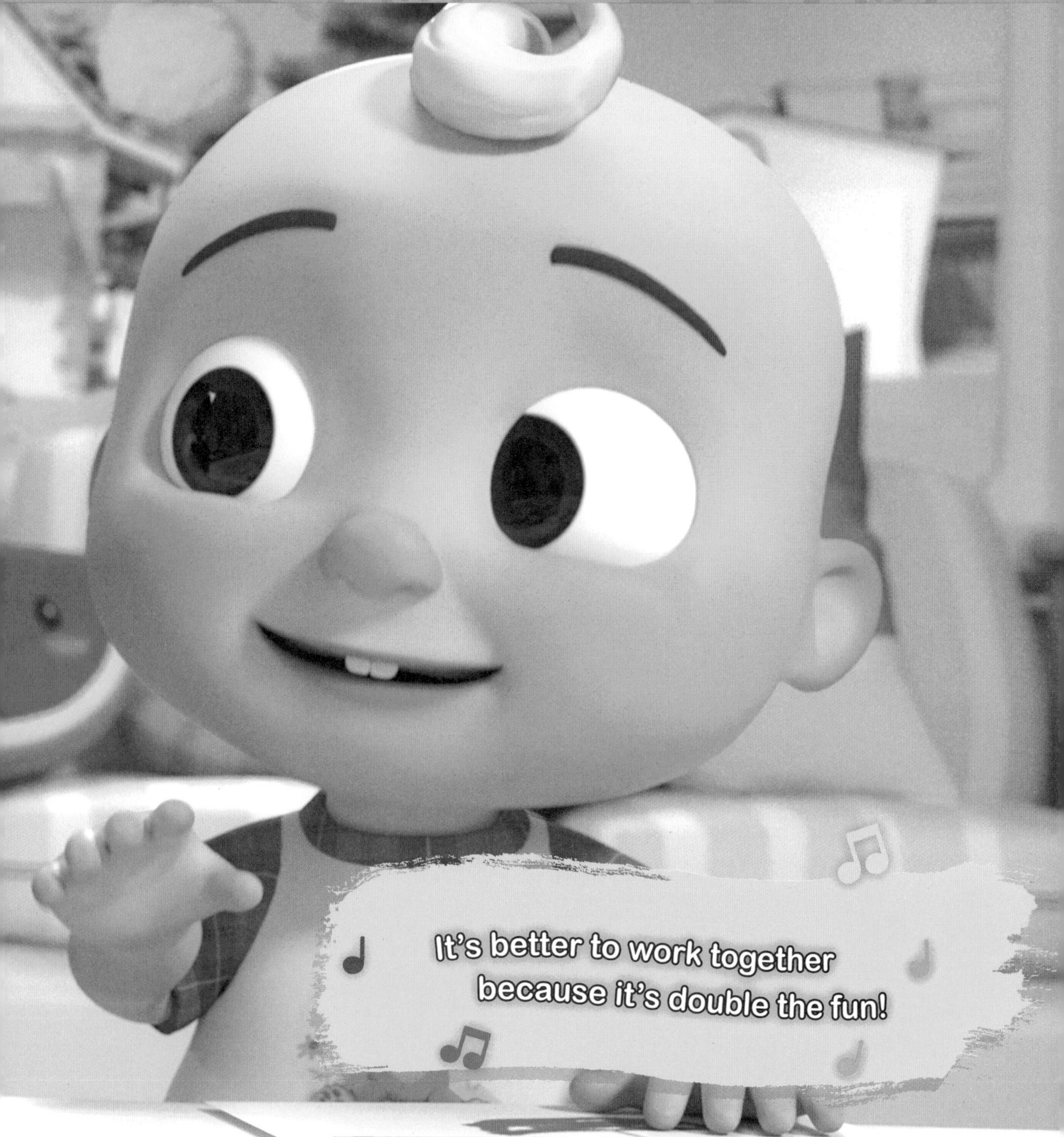

It's better to work together
because it's double the fun!

I have fun when you have fun! Yes!
Share when you only have one!

Today's our day to play
out here in the sun.
Riding on the tricycle!

When we work together,
everyone has more fun!

JJ and Cody will ride the tricycle together.

5, 4, 3, 2, 1 . . .

BLAST OFF!

It's better to work together
because it's double the fun!

I have fun when you have fun!
Yes!

Share when you
only have one!

Sharing is fun!

Thanks for learning how to share with us!

Thanks for reading with us!

See you soon!